TREE FU TOM

Tiny Tom

"Before starting any adventure, we need to do the moves that turn our magic powers on. Come on, join in.

TIME FOR TREE FU!

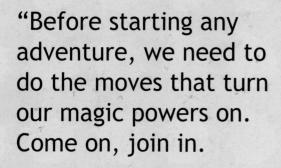

To make Tree Fu spells
do what you see . . .
Slide to the side,
and ***jump*** right back!
Hold your hands up high,
spin around . . .
Reach up for the sky!

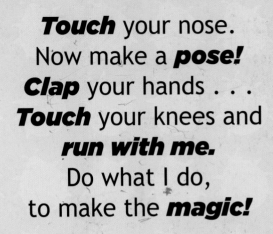

Touch your nose.
Now make a **pose!**
Clap your hands . . .
Touch your knees and
run with me.
Do what I do,
to make the **magic!**

Look, the
sapstone in my
belt is **glowing**.
Moving turned
our magic on."

One sunny day, Tom was looking for his friends.
"Twigs! Ariela! **HELLOOO!**" No one answered. "Where is
everyone?" he wondered.
Tom heard Ariela's whistle and he flew over to see her.
"Sorry Tom, no time to chat. I've got to go do this . . .
other thing," she said quickly before flying away.

It was the same with all of his friends, Zigzoo, Squirmtum and Twigs . . . they all said they were too busy to play.

"WHAT'S GOING ON?" said Tom.

Secretly, Tom's friends were all rushing off to the same place – Ariela's barn. It was Tom's birthday and they wanted to surprise him!
Zigzoo and Twigs placed a long, wrapped present on the table. "I feel as bad as a bear with an empty beehive for sending Tom away," said Ariela as she was hanging up some bunting.

"Don't worry, he'll be happy again when he sees his birthday cake and present," said Twigs.
"Speaking of Tom's present, I still need to finish my part of it – I'll be back soon!" said Zigzoo as he hurried back to his boat.

Everyone was so busy, they didn't see those naughty Mushas, Puffy and Stink, hiding outside the barn.

"Did you see the size of that present?" asked Stink.

"Oooh, I want it!" giggled Puffy, greedily. "But we need to stick to the plan."

"Fine," groaned Stink. "We'll stick with *the plan*. Er, what is the plan?"

Puffy sighed. "You're going to float over the ranch hanging on to this sparkly balloon filled with fireflies. While everyone is looking at you, I'll sneak behind them and steal the cake and present!"

"Ooh, it sounds like I am the **STAR** of this plan," said Stink, proudly.

"Yes, yes," huffed Puffy, impatiently. "You're the star."

Back at his boat, Zigzoo was busy finishing his part of Tom's present.
"Oh, this is going to be my best invention yet! And, best of all, it will make Tom's present extra-special," he said excitedly.

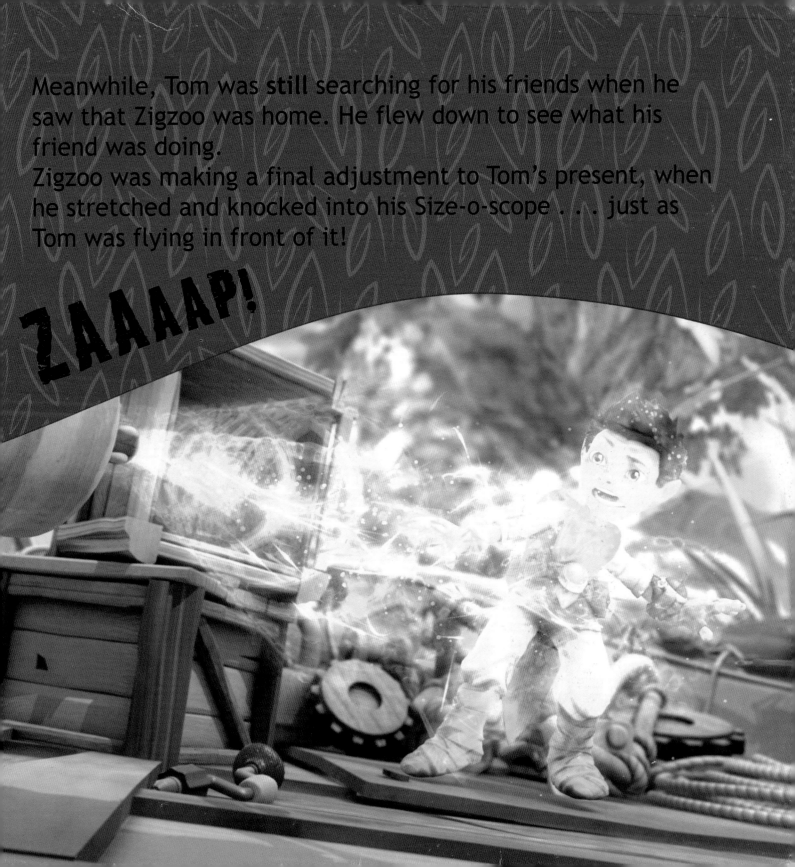

Meanwhile, Tom was **still** searching for his friends when he saw that Zigzoo was home. He flew down to see what his friend was doing.

Zigzoo was making a final adjustment to Tom's present, when he stretched and knocked into his Size-o-scope . . . just as Tom was flying in front of it!

ZAAAAP!

"Oh no," squeaked a very tiny Tom. "The Size-o-scope got me, I'm tiny!"
Tom was so tiny that Zigzoo didn't see him.
"Oh, my Size-o-scope!" cried Zigzoo, relieved. "It's lucky it didn't zap anything."
"But it did! Zigzoo, help! It zapped me! I'm here!" squeaked a teeny-tiny Tom.

Zigzoo carried on clattering around. Tom flew in front of Zigzoo, waving his arms in the air. "Look over here, Zigzoo! I've been shrunk!" shouted Tom. But he had to quickly dodge out of the way when Zigzoo nearly swatted him!

In this moment of danger, Tom was glad to hear a friendly voice calling out his name.

"TO-OOM!" shouted Twigs.

"Twigs!" Tom shouted loudly, as he flew in front of Twigs.

Ariela landed next to Twigs. "I thought I heard a squeaky voice saying, 'It's me, Tom!' but I can't see him," Twigs told her, sadly.

"We all feel bad, Twigs, but we had to stay away so we could get the surprise ready and show Tom how much we love him," Ariela said, comfortingly.

"They do like me after all!" thought Tom.

Suddenly, he heard the Mushas talking nearby.
"When those Treelings are looking at you flying over them holding this sparkly balloon, I'll swipe the present and cake," said Puffy.
"Ooh, the balloon is almost full of fireflies," laughed Stink.
"And here's the last one," said Puffy, grabbing hold of Flicker!

Tom spotted Flicker and raced to rescue him, but as Tom flew inside the balloon, Puffy tied the end, trapping them **both** inside!

Puffy tied Stink to the balloon and he soared into the sky.
"I'm a star!" Stink shouted to the Treelings down below.
"What a beautiful balloon!" called Squirmtum. "Wait, is
that Stink?"
Inside the balloon, Tom shouted and Flicker flashed his light to
try and get their friends' attention, but it was no good. While
everyone was distracted, Puffy crept into the barn and stole
Tom's present and cake.

"Puffy! How do I get down?" Stink shouted, seeing Puffy with the present and cake.

"You're not supposed to," Puffy laughed. "It's all for me!"

Stink started kicking his legs angrily, until the ropes tying him to the balloon began to snap. He fell, landing on top of Puffy!

The Mushas ran away in a panic, leaving the present and cake behind.

Meanwhile, the balloon was rising higher and higher into the sky . . .

Inside the balloon, Tom knew he was in trouble! "The balloon is floating up out of control and fast. To stop it, we'll have to **POP** it! It's time to do the *Super Arrow* spell. Are you ready?"

TREE FU GO!

"Copy me, into your spell pose."

"Release your back hand."

"Join hands and pull back."

"Shoot your hand out to the side."

"Hand by your foot, join hands."

"Pull back, aim high and release your back hand."

"Now clap and say 'Super Arrow!' to send the magic to me! 'Super Arrow!'"

"We did it! You saved us, thanks for your help!"

Tom jumped onto Flicker's back and flew
back down to his friends.
"Flicker!" cried Squirmtum, excitedly.
"What's that on your back?"
Zigzoo looked through his magnifying glass.
"It's Tom! Oh ribberty-roo, the
Size-o-scope must have zapped you earlier.
Don't worry, I can fix this!" said Zigzoo as
he hurried off to his boat.

ZAAAAPPP!

Zigzoo soon returned and Tom
stood in front of the Size-o-scope.
As Zigzoo pressed the button, Tom grew
and grew until he reached his normal size.
Twigs flew at Tom and gave him a **BIG** hug! "You're back!
And you're big!" he cried.

"Well," said Ariela, as she opened the barn doors, "we have one
more thing to say . . ."

"SURPRISE! HAPPY BIRTHDAY!"
"Wow, thanks! I thought you guys didn't want me around anymore . . ." Tom said.
"Sorry we acted funny, we wanted to do something extra special for your birthday," Ariela explained.
"Enough of this mushy stuff – open your present!" shouted Twigs, excitedly. So, Tom did – it was a brand-new leaf board!
"Thanks guys!"

"This gadget makes it a super leaf board and able to do super tricks!" explained Zigzoo. "Come on, Twigs, we've got to try this!" said Tom.

As Tom played on his new leaf board with Twigs, he shouted happily, "Waaahhooo! This is the best birthday **ever**!"

WAAAHHHOOO!

Thanks for helping me in Treetopolis, see you soon for another adventure. Bye for now!

TREE FU TOM:
TINY TOM
A BANTAM BOOK
978 0 857 51230 7

Published in Great Britain
by Bantam, an imprint of Random House
Children's Publishers UK
A Random House Group Company.

This edition published 2014

1 3 5 7 9 10 8 6 4 2

Tree Fu Tom created by Daniel Bays.
Based on the episode 'Tiny Tom', written by John Loy.
TREE FU TOM word and device marks are trade marks of the British Broadcasting
Corporation and FremantleMedia Limited and are used under licence.
TREE FU TOM device marks © BBC and FremantleMedia Limited MMX.
The "BBC" word mark and logo are trade marks of the British Broadcasting Corporation
and are used under licence. BBC Logo © BBC 1996. The "CBeebies" word mark and logo are
trade marks of the BBC and are used under licence. CBeebies Logo © BBC 2001.
Licensed by FremantleMedia Limited.
www.TreeFuGo.com

Bantam Books are published by Random House Children's Publishers UK,
61-63 Uxbridge Road, London W5 5SA

www.randomhousechildrens.co.uk

Addresses for companies within The Random House Group Limited can be found at:
www.randomhouse.co.uk/offices.htm

THE RANDOM HOUSE GROUP Limited Reg. No. 954009

A CIP catalogue record for this book is available
from the British Library

Printed in China

MIX
Paper from
responsible sources
FSC® C020056

The Random House Group Limited supports the Forest Stewardship Council® (FSC®), the leading international
forest-certification organisation. Our books carrying the FSC label are printed on FSC®-certified paper.
FSC is the only forest certification scheme endorsed by the leading environmental organizations, including Greenpeace
Our paper procurement policy can be found at www.randomhouse.co.uk/environment